Commu
Near and far

T0247221

VISTA®
HIGHER LEARNING

Boston, Massachusetts

SOCIAL STUDIES

Hey there, I'm Tim!

Hi, my name is André.

This is Tim, and this is André. Tim and André have a lot in common. They're both 17 years old and both are high school students. Like most teenagers, Tim and André have a lot of different hobbies. They like watching movies, playing sports, and just hanging out.

Tim and André are friends, but they don't see each other every day. In fact, they don't go to the same school or live in the same **community**. They don't even live in the same country!

Tim lives in Colorado, a state in the western part of the United States. The region is famous for its beautiful natural areas, including mountains and rivers.

André lives in São Paulo, which is the largest city in Brazil by **population**. It's the capital of the state of São Paulo and is known for its interesting attractions and **cultural diversity**.

However, Tim has never visited São Paulo, and André has never visited Colorado. They've never even met each other in person. So how can the two young men be friends?

Fort Morgan, Colorado

São Paulo, Brazil

Online pen pal programs help students around the world communicate. They write e-mails and send messages to each other.

Tim and André are online pen pals! They're taking part in a **program** for international communication. In the program, students at schools in different countries are pen pals. They **correspond** online and sometimes do projects together.

Tim's social studies teacher joined the program as a way for her students to learn more about different communities and cultures. André's teacher joined for similar reasons and arranged to partner with an American class. The class was the one Tim was in, and Tim and André were paired as pen pals.

One of their first **assignments** was to find out more about each other's lifestyles and communities. Tim got the assignment first and e-mailed André, who e-mailed back right away. Both teens were excited to work with a student from another country.

They started e-mailing to learn more about each other and their home countries. Soon they began **messaging** more and more often—both for their assignment and just for fun! It wasn't long before Tim and André became friends, despite some very big differences. Take a look at their message histories to learn just how different—and similar—their lives are!

9:39

Hi!

Hey, there!

What's up?

messaging

q w e r t y u i o p

a s d f g h j k l

So, tell me about where you live, André. I've always wanted to go to Brazil, but I've never been there.

Well, São Paulo is a really big, exciting city. It has a big population made up of different kinds of people from all sorts of **backgrounds**. It's actually known for its cultural diversity. It's also very **urban**, with lots of tall buildings and traffic, but I like it. There are so many things to see and do!

It sounds cool! What's your neighborhood like?

I live in a central part of São Paulo. It's a big neighborhood, and there are a lot of buildings and people. I live in a small apartment with my parents. There's a really beautiful park nearby and a lot of restaurants and cafés.

EXTRA!

**São Paulo
Neighborhoods**

*yellow = lower population
dark green = higher population*

Population density tells us how crowded a city or area is.
To find the population density of a town or city,
divide the total population by the area.

population of São Paulo* = 12,252,023 people

city area = 588 square miles (588 mi²) or 1,523 square
kilometers (1,523 km²)

population density = 20,837 people per square mile
(20,837/mi²) or 8,045 people per square kilometer (8,045/km²)

Fort Morgan is a small rural town in Colorado. The population density of Fort Morgan is about 2,338 people per square mile.

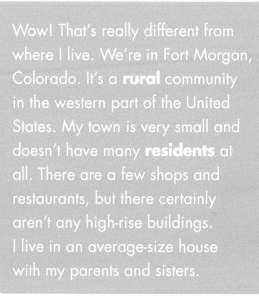

Wow! That's really different from where I live. We're in Fort Morgan, Colorado. It's a **rural** community in the western part of the United States. My town is very small and doesn't have many **residents** at all. There are a few shops and restaurants, but there certainly aren't any high-rise buildings. I live in an average-size house with my parents and sisters.

That sounds like a great place to live. It would be nice to have a house with a yard.

Yeah, it is. I like it a lot, but it would be fun to live in a big, exciting city, too.

9

So, how do you get to school? Do you ride your bike?

No way! I can't! My school is about three miles* from my apartment, and the streets around here are just too busy in the mornings. I take the subway, but we call it the metro here. I'm pretty lucky because there's a station right near our apartment. The metro system in São Paulo is huge and one of the busiest in South America. It's usually really crowded. It takes me about 30 minutes to get from my home to school, but it can take longer if it's really busy or if there are delays.

subway

Wow, that sounds complicated. My town is too small to have much **public transportation**. Most people use cars and bicycles to get around. I ride my bike to school. It's about three miles away as well, but it only takes me about 15 minutes to get there.

One mile is equal to 1.61 kilometers.

São Paulo subway map

Over 4.6 million people travel on the São Paulo metro every day.

So, what is there to do for fun in Fort Morgan?

 Oh, there's a lot of stuff to do here. Most people especially like to spend time outside. I like to run, read, and ski. I'm on the school basketball team, too, and that's really fun. How about you?

 Oh, basketball isn't so big in São Paulo. The big sport here is football, what you call soccer.

 Of course, how could I forget! LOL!

superhero

comic book

 When I'm not playing soccer, I read a lot. Most of the time I read comic books. São Paulo has some really cool comic book stores.

Hey! I like comic books, too! I collect them. I especially like the ones about superheroes.

 I like superhero comics, too! But my favorites are Japanese *manga*. They're awesome!

I really like them, too! Manga comic books are popular here. A lot of my friends read them. My aunt even brought back some manga from Japan when she went there for work.

 Cool! It would be great to see manga that are actually from Japan!

Comics Blog Videos Events

Japanese Manga

The word "manga" was first used around the eighteenth century, but it's a very old style of storytelling. The first manga appeared around the twelfth century. These old manga stories were usually about life in a Japanese community. Most of them were funny and used as an early form of entertainment.

Since then, manga has become an important part of Japanese culture and has gotten more popular internationally. Nowadays, Japanese manga are not only used to tell funny stories, they're used to tell every kind of story you can imagine. There are manga stories about action, adventure, comedy, drama, mystery, romance, and more. Modern manga are read by people of all ages and are often printed in black and white. This is usually done to help artists produce comics fast enough to keep up with fan demand!

Tim and André messaged more and more. As they corresponded, Tim and André made an interesting discovery. Although their lives were quite different, their interests were very similar. By the time their assignment was finished, they had become very good friends and thought it would be fun to meet.

Then, one day, Tim got an e-mail from André and it had exciting news!

To: Tim.Jones@VHLmail.co

From: André.Dias@SP-mail.co.br

Hi Tim,

You're never going to believe this, but my family is taking a trip to the United States this summer! We're visiting some friends in Southern California. We'll be traveling around the Los Angeles and San Diego areas. And guess what? We're going to a comic book **convention**. I'm so excited! I can't wait to see all of my favorite superheroes and meet other comic book fans. Any chance you and your family can come?

André

EXTRA!

Comic book conventions are big meetings for people who like comic books. Comic book fans go to learn about and buy comics, talk to people who make them, and meet other fans. It's a chance for them to listen to writers speak, learn more about their favorite characters, and find new comics to read. They often also **dress up** as their favorite characters and sometimes even act like them. The first comic book convention was held in New York City in 1964. Now there are comic book conventions all over the world.

Tim read André's e-mail and was just as excited about the trip. He had always wanted to go to a comic book convention, and it would be so much fun to meet André and his family!

Tim talked to his parents about the trip and the convention. He knew they were big comic book fans as well, so he thought they'd be interested—and they were! They started planning the trip and Tim e-mailed André immediately to tell him the big news.

To: André.Dias@SP-mail.co.br

From: Tim.Jones@VHLmail.co

Hey André,

I asked my parents, and they said yes! We're coming to the comic book convention, too. We can meet and go together!

Tim

André and Tim were very excited about the convention and about meeting each other. They knew that a lot of people in the comic book community would be there. It was going to be really fun to meet so many people who had the same interests.

The two friends started planning what they were going to do. There were so many speakers and events to choose from. It was going to take some time!

KNOW IT ALL

People use the word "community" in different ways. It sometimes means a group of people with the same interests. There can be sports communities, online communities, and comic book communities as well!

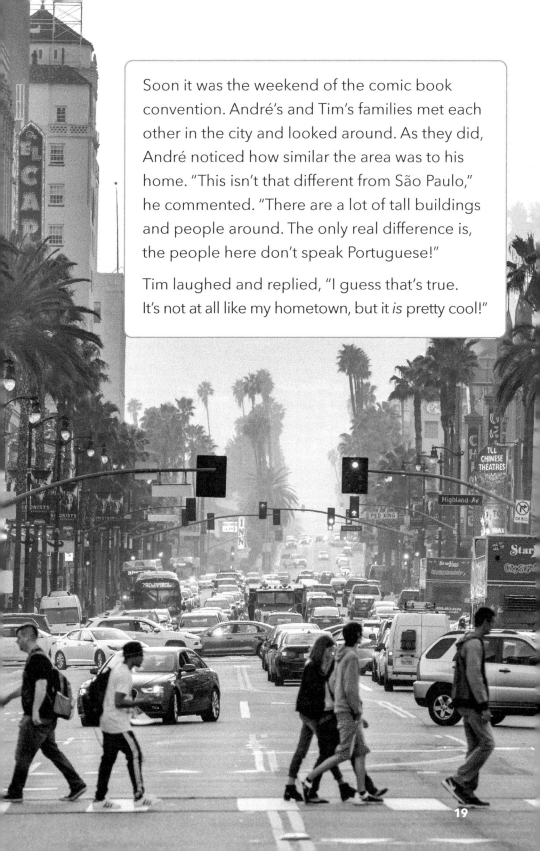

Soon it was the weekend of the comic book convention. André's and Tim's families met each other in the city and looked around. As they did, André noticed how similar the area was to his home. "This isn't that different from São Paulo," he commented. "There are a lot of tall buildings and people around. The only real difference is, the people here don't speak Portuguese!"

Tim laughed and replied, "I guess that's true. It's not at all like my hometown, but it *is* pretty cool!"

André and Tim had a wonderful time at the convention. They talked and laughed a lot. There were so many people there who were just like them—**crazy about** comics!

They got a chance to speak with some of the artists and writers who create comics. André saw a speaker who gave a talk about drawing superhero stories. There was even a manga artist there!

superhero costumes

Tim went to a costume contest. He said it was awesome. Next time he wants to wear one, too.

There was a writing contest as well, but Tim and André didn't have time to enter. There was just too much to do!

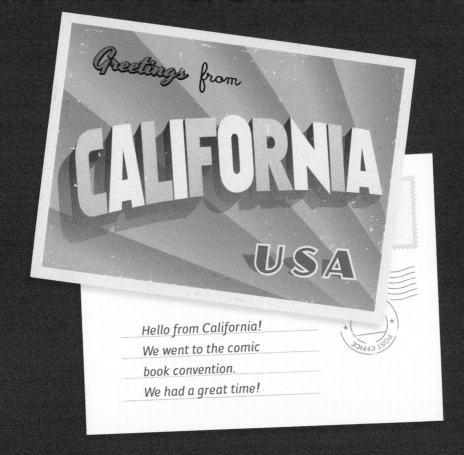

Greetings from
CALIFORNIA
USA

Hello from California!
We went to the comic
book convention.
We had a great time!

POST OFFICE

After their exciting weekend at the convention, it was soon time for Tim and André to say good-bye. They both had to start their long trips back home, but what a great few days they had. "Thanks for showing me part of the U.S.," said André.

"No problem," replied Tim. "I'd love to come visit you in São Paulo. It would be a great way to learn more about where you're from. Maybe we could call it 'homework'?"

"Yes!" said André laughing. "You have to come visit. We have a great comic book community in Brazil, too. Maybe you can come down to a convention there," he added.

"I'd love to," said Tim. "**Belonging** to a community is fun —especially the comic book community!"

What's your superhero name?

Choose one word from each list. Put the words together to create your superhero name!

Example: (List 1) + (List 2) + (List 3)
Brave   Star   Dancer

List 1 Pick your favorite color.

RED: Chosen   GREEN: Wonderful
ORANGE: Super   BLUE: Brave
YELLOW: Wild   **PURPLE**: Unstoppable

List 2 Pick your birth month.

JAN. Fox   **MAY** Night   **SEPT.** Fighting
FEB. Star   **JUNE** Horse   **OCT.** Speedy
MAR. Rainbow   **JULY** Wolf   **NOV.** Furry
APR. Sea   **AUG.** Strong   **DEC.** Rocket

List 3 Pick the letter of your first name.

A. Rescuer   **H.** Kid   **O.** Leader   **V.** Wind
B. Friend   **I.** Champion   **P.** Snake   **W.** Dragon
C. Dancer   **J.** Jumper   **Q.** Thing   **X.** Moon
D. Protector   **K.** Face   **R.** Brain   **Y.** Computer
E. Doctor   **L.** Master   **S.** Power   **Z.** Giant
F. Robot   **M.** Professor   **T.** Storm
G. Helper   **N.** Scientist   **U.** Shark

community a place where people live and work together; also a group of people with similar interests

population the number of people living in an area

cultural diversity the state of having a number of different groups, types, ethnic groups, and nationalities of people

program a set of activities to be done

correspond to communicate; to send messages back and forth

assignment a task or job to be done, usually for work or school

message (v.) to send written notes or pieces of information back and forth online

background a person's education, family life, and other personal experiences

urban of, in, or related to a city or town

population density a measure of the number of people who live in a set area

rural of, in, or related to a place not in a city

resident a person who lives in a city, town, or area

public transportation subway, train, and bus systems in a city

convention a meeting of people with similar hobbies, jobs, or other interests

dress up to put on crazy or unusual clothing for play or fun

be crazy about (something) to like something very much

belong to feel comfortable with a group of people or in a place; to be part of